PLEASE WASH
YOUR HANDS
BEFORE YOU READ ME
AND KEEP ME CLEAN

The Let's Talk Library™

Let's Talk About
Living in a Blended Family

Elizabeth Weitzman

The Rosen Publishing Group's
PowerKids Press™
New York

Published in 1996 by The Rosen Publishing Group, Inc.
29 East 21st Street, New York, NY 10010

First Edition

Book design: Erin McKenna

Photo credits: Cover © G + M David de Lossy/Image Bank; p. 19 © Laurie Bayer/International Stock; all other photos by Seth Dinnerman.

Weitzman, Elizabeth.
    Let's talk about living in a blended family / Elizabeth Weitzman. — 1st ed.
        p.   cm. — (The let's talk library)
    Includes index.
    Summary: Provides advice on how to accept and deal with the challenges of living in a stepfamily or blended family.
    ISBN 0-8239-2312-6
    1. Stepfamilies—Juvenile literature. [1. Stepfamilies.] I. Title. II. Series.
HQ759.92.W45 1996
646.7'8—dc20   96-3334
                                                                           CIP
                                                                           AC

Manufactured in the United States of America

Table of Contents

Laura

Laura's parents **divorced** (dih-VORST) when she was only two. For many years she and her mother did everything together. But when Laura was eight, her mother began dating a man named Jeff. Jeff was always nice to Laura, but when he was around, Laura sometimes felt left out. When her mother and Jeff decided to get married, Laura was angry and unhappy.

◀ You might feel angry, scared, or sad that your life is going to change when your mom gets married.

5

What Is a Blended Family?

Many kids live with only one parent—a single parent. Sometimes a single parent meets another adult that he or she really likes. They may date for a while. Then they may decide to get married.

When two single parents marry, they join their families together. Then they have a blended family or a stepfamily. This is a big change.

6

It may take some time to get to know your new family. ▶

Remarriage

It's not easy when a parent gets married again. It means there's no chance that your parents will get back together. You may feel that one parent is **deserting** (dih-ZERT-ing) the other. And the parent who's getting married is probably busy planning the wedding. You may feel angry, sad, jealous, or scared. That is because your whole world seems to be changing. Ask to spend some special time alone with your parent. Use this time to tell her how you feel.

◀ Ask your mom if you can spend some time alone with her.

Stepparents

There are going to be a lot of changes after your dad gets married. The biggest one will be getting to know a new parent—your **stepparent** (STEP-parent). Some kids decide to hate their stepmoms without giving them a chance. But you already know you share one thing with your stepmom: You both love your dad. So do your best to get to know her. And remember, she's trying too. You might even make a new friend.

Some kids decide they don't like their new stepmom before they even get to know her. ▶

New Rules

You'll probably have to get used to different rules once your parent gets remarried. This may seem unfair to you.

Instead of getting mad about these changes, talk about them. Tell your mom and stepdad how you feel. They may not change the rules, but at least you'll understand why they've made them. If you treat your mom and your stepdad with respect, they'll respect you too.

◄ Talking to your mom and your stepdad can help you understand why they made the rules they did.

Stepbrothers and Stepsisters

A new family often means new brothers and sisters. It may seem like there's less room and attention for you. But more brothers and sisters also means there's always someone around for advice or company. Look for a spot in your home that can be all yours. Ask your dad to help you keep this area private. This way you'll have somewhere to go when you want to be by yourself.

Having a new stepsister is a ▶ chance to make a new friend.

A New Home

After your parent gets remarried, you may have to move to a new house, or even a new city. You don't have to lose your friends because you're leaving. You can always write, and maybe even visit. Moving just gives you the chance to make more friends.

Try to unpack as soon as you get to your new home. You'll feel much better when you're surrounded by familiar things, like posters and your stuffed animals.

◀ Sometimes it's hard to get used to a new place.

New Feelings

You'll have lots of new **emotions** (ee-MOE-shuns) when your mom remarries. You might feel as if you are **betraying** (be-TRAY-ing) your dad if you love your stepdad. Or you might feel left out because your baby step-brother takes up so much of your mom's time. Share your feelings with someone else. If your mom is busy, try talking to a friend, your teacher, or another adult. Or try talking to your stepbrother or stepsister. They've been through the same changes you have.

18

One way to deal with all these new feelings is to spend some time with your mom or dad. ▶

Halfsisters and Halfbrothers

Your dad and stepmom may have a baby together. This child will be your **halfbrother** (HAF-brother) or **halfsister** (HAF-sister). You may feel jealous of the new baby when it receives a lot of attention. Tell your dad how you feel. Then offer to help. It will be fun to get to know your new brother or sister. And remember: Even though your dad will love the new baby, he'll still care just as much about you.

◀ You can help take care of your
new halfbrother.

21

A Real Family

It takes a while for a group of people to blend together into a real family. When parents get remarried, there are a lot of changes for everyone to accept. At first, a new family means more sharing, more noise, and less space. But with time, you'll find that it also means more friends, more fun, and eventually, more love.

Glossary

betray (be-TRAY) To be disloyal.

desert (dih-ZERT) To leave someone forever.

divorce (dih-VORS) When two people end a marriage.

emotion (ee-MOE-shun) Feelings.

halfbrother (HAF-brother) Your brother by your parent and your stepparent.

halfsister (HAF-sister) Your sister by your parent and your stepparent.

stepparent (STEP-parent) Your parent's new husband or wife.

Index